Dear Parent:
Your child's love of read

Every child learns to read in a differe[nt]
speed. Some go back and forth between reading levels a..
favorite books again and again. Others read through each level in
order. You can help your young reader improve and become more
confident by encouraging his or her own interests and abilities. From
books your child reads with you to the first books he or she reads
alone, there are I Can Read Books for every stage of reading:

SHARED READING
Basic language, word repetition, and whimsical illustrations,
ideal for sharing with your emergent reader

BEGINNING READING
Short sentences, familiar words, and simple concepts
for children eager to read on their own

READING WITH HELP
Engaging stories, longer sentences, and language play
for developing readers

READING ALONE
Complex plots, challenging vocabulary, and high-interest topics
for the independent reader

ADVANCED READING
Short paragraphs, chapters, and exciting themes
for the perfect bridge to chapter books

I Can Read Books have introduced children to the joy of reading
since 1957. Featuring award-winning authors and illustrators and a
fabulous cast of beloved characters, I Can Read Books set the
standard for beginning readers.

A lifetime of discovery begins with the magical words **"I Can Read!"**

*Visit www.icanread.com for information
on enriching your child's reading experience.*

I Can Read Book® is a trademark of HarperCollins Publishers.

Batman: Dino Dilemma
Copyright © 2017 DC Comics.
BATMAN and all related characters and elements © & ™ DC Comics.
(s17)

HARP37267
Manufactured in U.S.A. No part of this book may be used or reproduced in any manner whatsoever without written permission except in the case of brief quotations embodied in critical articles and reviews. For information address HarperCollins Children's Books, a division of HarperCollins Publishers, 195 Broadway, New York, NY 10007.
www.icanread.com

Library of Congress Control Number: 2016952951
ISBN 978-0-06-236091-5

Book design by Erica De Chavez

17 18 19 20   LSCC   10 9 8 7 6 5 4 3 2   ❖ First Edition

BATMAN™

DINO DILEMMA

by Donald Lemke
illustrated by Andie Tong

Batman created by Bob Kane with Bill Finger

HARPER
An Imprint of HarperCollinsPublishers

BATMAN

Batman is an expert martial artist, crime fighter, and inventor. He is known as the World's Greatest Detective.

BATGIRL

Barbara Gordon fights alongside Batman using high-tech gadgets and martial-arts skills. Her father, James Gordon, does not know her secret identity as Batgirl.

NIGHTWING

The original Robin, Dick Grayson grew up and became the hero Nightwing. He protects a city near Gotham and sometimes helps Batman.

THE RIDDLER

Edward Nigma turned his love of puzzles into a life of crime. As the Riddler, this super-villain wields a question-mark cane and asks clever riddles.

Five students entered Gotham City's
Natural History Museum.
Their science fair projects
had earned them each a ticket
to a brand-new dinosaur exhibit.

A guide led the prize-winners
past rare dinosaur fossils.
"A raptor!" yelled one student,
pointing at a sharp-clawed skeleton.

A spray-painted message read:
"What dinosaur is a real
blast from the past?"
A high-tech explosive hung nearby.
"Dino-mite!" the guide shouted,
and then pulled an alarm.

Moments later, three super heroes
burst into the museum.
Nightwing calmed the students
as his partners spotted the dynamite.
"How long till we're—" Batman began.
"Extinct?" Batgirl finished.

Batgirl studied the explosive.

"This is a real puzzle," she said.

"You mean riddle?" Nightwing asked.

The hero pointed at a large purple

question mark on another wall.

"The Riddler," Batman growled.
Painted near the question mark was
a second clue from the villain.
"Where does a triceratops sit
in a museum?" it read.

A student slowly raised her hand.

"On its tricera-bottom," she said.

The frightened students giggled.

"Of course!" Batman said.

Ka-boom!

The dynamite suddenly exploded.

Batman and Batgirl shielded

the students with their capes.

The floor shook like an earthquake,

rattling the dinosaur displays.

"This way!" Nightwing shouted.

He led the group to the next room.

There was a giant

triceratops skeleton.

The Riddler had painted

a third clue next to it:

"Where was the T. rex when

the lights went out?"

A shy boy bravely spoke up,

"He was in the dark!"

Click!

The museum lights went out.

The students screamed.

Smash!

Bones crashed to the floor.

The group ran as dinosaur skeletons

crumbled around them.

They stopped at the T. rex display.

There was another clue:

"What dinosaur has many plates

but never eats off one?"

"That's easy!" said an excited girl.

She looked at the other students.

"Stegosaurus!" they yelled.

The super heroes smiled

but didn't have time to celebrate.

Wham! A giant T. rex tooth stuck

into the floor like a sword.

The super heroes looked up.

More razor-sharp teeth rattled

loose from the skeleton's jaws.

The Dark Knight quickly removed
a Batarang from his Utility Belt.
He flung the metal weapon
and knocked a falling tooth aside.
Nightwing and Batgirl did the same.

Then the super heroes hurried
everyone to the stegosaurus display.
They followed the skeleton's
backbone to the tip of its tail.
"Another clue!" a student cried out.

"What two things spell the end
of a dinosaur?" Batman read.

The students thought in silence.

Batgirl kneeled and pointed
at the last two letters in the clue.

"U-R," Batgirl spelled aloud.

"Yes, you are!" shouted a voice.

The super heroes spun around.

The Riddler stood behind them,

holding his question-mark cane.

"We have a bone to pick with you,"
Nightwing told the villain.
"Just one?" the Riddler asked.
He held up a bag of bones and
pulled out one from a raptor.

"Without these pieces, you'll never solve my greatest puzzle."
The Riddler pointed at the exhibit. Hundreds of bones covered the floor like a giant jigsaw puzzle.

The Riddler dropped the bone and
raised his question-mark cane.

Bzzzt!

He fired an electric bolt
at the super heroes.

Nightwing flipped out of the way.

The deadly bolt struck

the pterodactyl display overhead.

"Look out!" shouted Batgirl

as the skeleton fell from above.

Batman and Batgirl shot
their grapnel guns at the ceiling.
They gathered the students under
their arms and swung safely away.

Smash! The pterodactyl skeleton crashed down on the Riddler, trapping him in its giant rib cage. "Get me out of this bird!" he said.

"A pterodactyl isn't a bird,"
a student told the Riddler.
"It's only a reptile."
"I tell the riddles around here,
kid!" the villain shot back.

The Gotham City Police arrived.

"Don't worry," said Batman

as they put the Riddler in cuffs.

"You'll have plenty of time

to bone up on dino facts in jail!"

The super heroes stared at
the mess of bones on the floor.
"How do we solve this final puzzle?"
Nightwing asked his partners.
"That's easy," Batman replied,
pointing at the smiling students.
"With a little help."